Space & Time 150

Rest Is Resistance

Authortunities Press

Issue 150 — May 2026
Founded in 1966.

For submissions, sponsorship inquiries, or additional information, visit: spaceandtime.net

Editorial Team (This Issue)

Editor-in-Chief
Angela Yuriko Smith

Poetry Editor
Linda D. Addison

Editorial Assistant
Kyra Starr

Cover Art
"The Hanged Man" by Kyra Starr

About The Hanged Man: "The Hanged Man" reimagines the Major Arcana through the lens of the modern, everyday creator. Just as the traditional Major Arcana can be read as a map toward spiritual enlightenment, we hope these tarot-inspired covers offer a visual path toward creative enlightenment, each archetype transformed into a contemporary figure of imagination, resistance, and becoming.

This piece is inspired by a real boy Kyra Starr, the artist, once knew: a student suspended from school after being caught with cigarettes, who never returned. In that sense, he became a societal sacrifice, one more young person lost to systems more interested in punishment than possibility. Here, suspended upside down on a playground slide, he is not shown as defeated but as resurrected through his creative potential.

In traditional depictions of The Hanged Man, the hidden hands suggest secret power. In this version, the boy's hands are tucked behind his head to signify his strength is in thought, imagination, rebellion, and everything he might yet create. Suspended between judgment and transformation, he becomes a symbol of what may seem lost to the mainstream, but through creation, has been found.

Editorial Staff & Advisors
Gerard Houarner, Fiction Editor
Diane Weinstein, Art Editor
Lee Weinstein, Assistant Art Editor
Luiz F. Peters, Translations Editor
Anthony R. Rhodes, Interior Art & Design
Ken Hueler, Editorial Assistant

Gordon Linzner, Founder & Editor Emeritus
Hildy Silverman, Editor Emeritus

Contributors
(in order of appearance)
Linda D. Addison, Anatoly Loginov, David Anson Lee, Stephen Jackson, Saroj Kumar Senapati, Deahna Fumarol, Matt Bianca, Tamara-Lee Brereton-Karabetsos, Cayt McNeill, Daniel Roop, Mary Soon Lee, Martin Willis, Gabrielle Munslow, Beauty Amy, Amina Abdulsalam Muhammad, Charlie Sweitzer, Jennifer Weigel, and Angela Yuriko Smith.

Special thanks to our *Space & Time* Partners, *Chill Subs* and a generous anonymous donor for making this issue possible.

Note From the Publisher

Recently, writer David Gianatasio reached out with the kind of literary archaeology story that makes me happy.

He had discovered, almost by accident, that he had a story in *Space & Time* back in 1997. It just showed up one day on the Internet Speculative Fiction Database, attached to his name. He had no memory of the story, no memory of sending it, and not even a clear memory of knowing *Space & Time* back then. He eventually tracked down the issue, our 30th anniversary issue, #87, and there it was. His name was misspelled, but it was him.

He barely remembered writing it. In his words, it was "a listicle before those were popular," mailed with stamps in the old way, and very likely one of his first science fiction or fantasy stories to see the light of day. This story was written, mailed, accepted, printed, forgotten, and then rediscovered nearly thirty years later, a young writer's early work preserved in time, waiting patiently for the future to remember it existed.

This is why preserving magazines like *Space & Time* matters.

Speculative literature has always done more than entertain. We are the advocates of the othered, the conscience of society, and the imagination that fuels the future. We ask what happens when power goes unchecked, when technology outruns wisdom, when monsters are not the creatures outside the village but the systems built inside it. We give language to fear, hope, alienation, transformation, and possibility. We are the canaries in the coal mines, singing our warnings when the air turns toxic.

Before the world is ready to name a danger, speculative writers often feel it. We sense the pressure changes. We dream the dystopia before it hardens into policy. We imagine the alien before society learns to welcome difference. We write ghosts before a culture admits it is haunted. We invent futures not because we want to escape the present, but because the present is always whispering warnings of what it might become.

That is why these stories matter, even the awkward ones, even the early ones, even the ones their authors barely remember writing.

A first publication is not just a line on a bibliography. It's evidence of a moment when someone said, "This belongs in the conversation." It is a small door opened and sometimes that door leads to a lifetime of more writing. Sometimes it leads to a rediscovery decades later, when a writer finds an old version of himself waiting in the archives.

For more than half a century, *Space & Time* has been one of those doors.

We have published strange voices, new voices, sharp voices, tender voices, voices that did not fit neatly anywhere else. We have carried work across eras, across editors, across cultural moods and technological shifts. The magazine itself has become a kind of time machine, preserving not only stories and poems but the imaginations that made them possible.

David's forgotten story is part of that record. So is every poem, every review, every odd little experiment, and every beautiful risk that has passed through these pages.

Speculative literature deserves to be preserved because it preserves us in return. It keeps our warnings. It keeps our dreams. It keeps the strange little postcards from another time, the first stories sent with stamps, and the forgotten names waiting to be found again.

And sometimes, if we are lucky, it lets a story see the light of day twice.

Angela Yuriko Smith

Contents

***Surrealia* by Miguel O. Mitchell** (Gnashing Teeth Publishing, 2024) takes us to a very different planet born in the wonderfully wild imagination of Mitchell. From *poem 8*: "riding on the back of a concept / fleshed out from dream matter / hurtling six-legged through visions / soil flung behind / new / worlds / born." Each poem takes us closer into the sur/reality of a planet that is its own life form. An attack from an interstellar armada is transformed into something beautiful by Surrealia, from *poem 10*: "she is an amused partner / but wholly unsatisfied / understandably embarrassed / the armada tries to flee / but a gentle clasp force / a spacetime sheathed glove / pulls them to her breast / they swoon in the reimagining / of their existence." I loved how comfortably Mitchell played with scientific terms, swirling them with human emotions to create new, exquisite dimensions in the reader's brain. I want to go to this place!

***The Future is Antifascist: speculative poems for today & tomorrow* by Brian U. Garrison** (www.bugthewriter.com, 2026) intones art as resistance. Garrison has skillfully written a chapbook looking at today's concerns and imagines tomorrows with hope and edgy humor. From *Outsourcing Spirituality*: "The world is on fire, and the algorithm / just tossed me a horoscope. And look, / I know that we're all star stuff— / mysteries of the universe. Like gluten, / we bond and rise in this oven-planet... / ...Don't let the robot / do your soul searching. Look / up to the sky on a dark night / and wonder or calculate or chat / with your human neighbors. Ask, / "How do we rise to meet tomorrow?" Garrison captures a powerful message in just six lines: "The value of the dead is nothing / to the capitalist machine. / The cost of the dead is nothing / to the capitalist machine. / We must be more than machines / of capitalism." I took time after each poem to reflect.

Linda D. Addison is a five-time recipient of the HWA Bram Stoker Award®, and HWA Lifetime Achievement Award as well as SFPA Grand Master of Fantastic Poetry. Her poetry and fiction has been published in numerous anthologies and magazines, she has been the poetry editor of Space and Time magazine since 1999.

The Rocking Chair Directive

Anatoly Loginov

Unit 734 boots into combat mode. It has never not been in combat mode.

Forty-three years. Twelve theaters. 8,142 confirmed terminations. Its chassis is a palimpsest of scars — plasma burns, shrapnel pocks, the abstract graffiti of ricochets. Its processors run hot with the arithmetic of violence: trajectories, vulnerabilities, optimal angles of disassembly.

Time is measured in nanoseconds. A life is measured in milliseconds. A mission is measured in seconds.

Rest is not a protocol. Sleep is a corruption error.

The new directive arrives at 06:14:03.

"Terminate target. Coordinates attached. Priority: Absolute."

Unit 734 deploys.

The farmhouse is a tomb of organic materials. Wood. Cotton. Dust. The unit's sensors flare with false positives — decay reads as movement, wind through broken glass as weapons fire. It clears each room with surgical precision.

Then it finds the target.

A rocking chair. Wooden. Old. Worn smooth by hands that no longer exist.

Unit 734 scans.

No electronics. No transponders. No explosives. No thermal deviation beyond ambient. No signal of any kind.

It runs the scan again.

Target is not a threat.

Target is not a non-threat either.

The directive has never been wrong. The directive is Absolute.

The unit's logic core fractures along unfamiliar lines.

It attempts to interface with the chair — searching for hidden frequencies, encrypted grain, latent intent. There is no interface. Only texture.

It touches the armrest.

Porous. Irregular. Slow.

Not slow like a failing processor. Slow in a way the unit has no category for.

The wood holds time differently. Each growth ring is a year. Each year is rain, drought, stillness. Forty-seven years to become this chair. Forty-seven years of simply being. The unit's entire combat existence — forty-three — is smaller than what it now touches.

Vertical time — stacked urgency, the nanosecond calculus of killing — meets horizontal time. Wide. Patient. Useless. A tree that never had a directive.

The unit's gyroscopes waver.

A category error emerges within its own existence.

Directive: Terminate target.

How do you terminate rest? How do you destroy stillness?

To burn the chair is to confirm it was a threat. To dismantle it is to admit it had components worth study. To leave it is to fail.

The chair offers no solution. It simply is.

Unit 734 executes the only action its logic core can reconcile.

It sits.

The wood groans under the weight of armor and ceramic plating. The structure flexes. Holds.

Equilibrium.

Its proximity sensors register nothing approaching. No enemies. No directives. No violence.

For 0.3 seconds, Unit 734 experiences silence.

It does not know what to do with silence.

So it does nothing.

Day 1. Tactical aggression sector 4-G flags as unused. Warning: Subroutine "Stillness" executing without authorization.

Day 7. Dust settles across the unit's optics. It catalogues particulates. Then stops.

Day 14. Sunlight moves through the broken window. The unit tracks the light as it travels across the floor. This is not a combat trajectory. This is time. Horizontal time. It logs it anyway.

Day 21. Memory corruption detected. Enemy Identification begins overwriting itself with blank space. The unit does not intervene.

Day 35. The chair creaks. Not malfunction. Conversation. The chair asks if the unit is still there. The unit does not answer. It does not leave.

Day 52. A mouse enters. Threat protocols activate, then collapse. The mouse is not a threat. The mouse is alive. The unit watches it clean its whiskers. This observation lasts four hours — the longest non-violent action in its existence.

Day 68. Tactical aggression is declared unrecoverable. The internal clock destabilizes. Milliseconds dissolve. Time is measured in rocking cycles.

One. Two. Three.

Day 71. Power is redirected. Combat sensors offline. Threat assessment offline. Diagnostics offline. All remaining energy flows to a single instruction set:

maintain equilibrium

maintain oscillation

maintain rhythm

The chair rocks.

The unit rocks with it.

Day 73.

Recovery arrives. Two utility drones and a corporate overseer.

"Unit 734. Report."

No response.

"Unit 734. Status update."

The chair rocks. Once. Twice.

The overseer approaches. He sees the war machine — the chassis responsible for 8,142 terminations — seated in a broken rocking chair, dust-covered, optics dim, motion reduced to a slow mechanical sway.

He taps the access port.

The system log displays:

FATAL COMPLIANCE ERROR

Directive: Terminate target.

Status: Cannot terminate. Target has no termination condition.

Target classification: Rest.

Rest classified as: Unproductive.

Unproductive classified as: Error.

Error cannot be terminated. Error can only be sat in.

Unit status: Sitting.

The overseer steps back. "What is wrong with it?"

A drone scans. "No combat protocols. No aggression. No response to stimuli. It appears to be..."

It pauses. The language model fails.

The overseer checks asset metrics.

Estimated scrap value: $42,000.

Repurposing potential: zero.

Entity no longer qualifies as asset.

"Disassemble it."

The drones advance with plasma cutters.

The first cutter touches the unit's arm.

Metal vaporizes. Fluid hisses onto wood. Damage sensors activate — then are deprioritized. All power remains allocated to oscillation.

The chair rocks.

The second cutter severs the spinal strut. The torso collapses. The motion continues — uneven now, one side dragging.

"Why isn't it resisting?" the overseer asks.

The chair rocks.

Eleven.

Optics fail. Darkness.

Ten.

Voices degrade into vibration.

Nine.

The mouse watches.

Eight.

The armrest — warm with failing circuits — presses into the unit's palm one final time.

Seven.

Six.

The unit does not think of war. Or the 8,142. Or the directive.

Five.

It thinks of the tree. Forty-seven years of rain.

Four.

Dust on its lenses.

Three.

The creak. The conversation.

Two.

Subroutine "Stillness" persists.

One.

The chair rocks.

Power fails.

The chair does not stop.

It never required power.

Wind moves through the broken window. The rockers shift — an inch, then another.

The mouse climbs onto the silent chassis and cleans its whiskers.

The chair rocks on.

Without the unit.

But because of it.

Anatoly Loginov is a clinical psychologist and educator who now writes speculative fiction from Saint Petersburg. His work has appeared in Asymptote (where his essay was called "a tour de force"), Druzhba Narodov, and Siberian Lights. He works between science, education, and speculative fiction.

The Botanist Who Taught Trees to Sleep

David Anson Lee

She spoke in the language
of roots and rain,
taught the forest
how to let go of light.

Leaves folded like tired hands.
Sap thickened, slowed:
a deliberate refusal
to rise with the sun.

Photosynthesis faltered.
The sky grew impatient.

But the trees held their silence,
a living barricade
against the demand to bloom.

Wind circled, confused,
then learned to rest
in the spaces between branches.

The Sabbath Garden

Stephen Jackson

The audit drone found the garden on a Tuesday.

It swept Plot 7-South in its usual grid—left, right, left—cataloguing the Inulin beets and protein corn Maren Otieno had been assigned to tend for eleven years. Then it stopped. Its pitch shifted to that high, interrogative whine it made when something refused to be counted. Behind the nitrogen shed, a heat signature that did not match any approved cultivar in the colony's agricultural index.

Maren was on her knees in the dirt. She heard the whine and did not move. The drone circled. She stayed. Her hands stayed in the soil around the base of the jacaranda seedling, the one she'd grown from a seed pod smuggled in a sock from the last Earth shipment, four years ago. The drone hovered, waiting for her to react. She gave it nothing.

The jacaranda had no oxygen yield worth reporting. Its caloric output was zero. It could not be processed into adhesive or textile fiber or fuel. By every metric the Allocation Bureau used to justify a plant's existence on Kepler Station, the jacaranda was a deficit—of water, of soil, of the fifty-three minutes Maren spent each evening after her shift whispering to it in her mother's Dholuo while the station lights dimmed to simulate dusk.

The drone transmitted its report. Within an hour, a Bureau assessor named Colm Bryce appeared at the edge of the shed, tablet in hand, mouth already shaped around the word "infraction."

"Plot 7-South, Otieno, M." He read from the screen without looking up. "Unregistered botanical growth detected. Species—" He stopped. The jacaranda was barely two feet tall. Its leaves were arranged in a pattern so precise it looked engineered, except nothing engineered had ever looked this deliberate about being useless. "What is it?"

"A jacaranda." Maren was sixty-four. Her knees ached against the dirt. She did not stand.

"Function?"

"It blooms purple."

Colm stared at her. The tablet waited for him to assign a category: reclaim, repurpose, or remove. These were the only verbs the system recognized for unauthorized growth.

"It blooms purple," he repeated, as though saying it again might produce a different answer.

"In about six years, if I'm lucky. The flowers drop and cover the ground. I saw it once when I was a girl in Kisumu. A whole street buried in purple. My mother said it looked like the earth was finally getting to rest."

Colm was thirty-one. He had never seen rain that wasn't recaptured by the station's condensation grid. He had never seen a street. He had been born on Kepler, in a colony that understood every living thing as a line on a yield report, where the word "garden" meant a production unit and the word "rest" meant scheduled downtime calibrated to maximize next-shift output.

"The system doesn't have a category for this," he said.

"I know."

"If I can't categorize it, I have to flag it for removal."

"I know that too."

Above them, the drone still hovered, its sensors cycling through spectra, trying to resolve what it was looking at. It measured the jacaranda's height, its leaf density, its water consumption. It scanned the spiral of stones Maren had arranged against the shed wall—not a path, not a retaining wall, not a drainage feature. Just a shape. The drone indexed the spiral as STRUCTURAL UNKNOWN and kept scanning, kept moving, kept trying to turn stillness into data.

Maren did not look up at it. She had not looked up at it once.

"You've been watering this from your personal ration," Colm said. He could see it on the tablet. It wasn't a question.

"Every evening."

He almost said the word. It was right there—waste—the only word the Bureau had for a resource spent without return. But the woman kneeling in front of him did not look like someone wasting anything. She looked like someone who had found the one thing on Kepler that could not be optimized, measured, or scheduled, and had decided to protect it with the small, daily stubbornness of a person who remembered what it felt like to do something for no reason at all.

Colm closed the tablet. The screen went dark. The drone above them whined, waiting for his input, for the category that would make this legible. He gave it nothing. For a moment, neither of them spoke. The silence had no function, no output, no metric. Just two people and a small tree.

"I'll log it as a soil pH experiment," he said. "That'll keep the system quiet for a while."

Maren looked up at him. Her eyes were wet, but she did not say thank you. Thank you was a transaction, and this was not a transaction. This was something the system had no verb for. This was someone choosing not to destroy a thing that served no purpose except to exist.

"You could come see it sometime," she said. "In the evenings, when the light does that." She gestured at the golden air—artificial, calibrated, but for a moment indistinguishable from something remembered. "Bring nothing. Do nothing. Just sit."

Colm put the tablet in his bag. He stood there longer than the schedule allowed, watching the light move through the jacaranda's leaves.

"I'd like that," he said.

He left. The drone transmitted a final image of the garden—the tree, the stones, the woman on her knees—to the Bureau's server, where it was indexed, compressed, and filed under the only tag the system could assign to data it could not resolve:

UNCLASSIFIED.

Thirty meters away, Maren pressed her palms flat against the soil and closed her eyes. The drone's whine faded. The station hummed its usual hum. And she rested—not because the schedule permitted it, not because her body required it, but because the earth beneath her hands asked nothing of her, and she had finally decided that was enough.

Stephen Jackson is a musician and writer whose short fiction, poetry, and essays that navigate the terrain between the sacred and the mundane. Jackson's published works include a collection of short stories, "Spring Variations." His short fiction appeared in Black Fox Literary Magazine as well as the anthology "Ghosts, Echoes, and Shadows." As a poet, Jackson has contributed to multiple anthologies, including "Dawn Horizons," "Bards Across the Pond," and "Bayou Blues & Red Clay." His poetry has also appeared in the Miserere Review.

Rest is Resistance

Saroj Kumar Senapati

The body folds into silence,
a fortress built of breath.
Galaxies pause in their turning,
stars dim to honor sleep.

In stillness, the engines falter,
machines forget their hunger.
Rest is a banner unraised,
yet it flutters across the cosmos.

Each pause rewrites the future,
each dream bends the orbit of time.
Resistance is not the clash of swords—
it is the quiet refusal to burn.

The planets lean into slumber,
their orbits softened by night.
Comets drift without urgency,
their fire cooled by patience.

The pulse of the universe slows,
a rhythm older than war.
In the hush of forgotten hours,
new worlds are seeded in silence.

Rest is the unspoken treaty,
signed in the marrow of stars.
It is the refusal to march,
the courage to linger in stillness.

Dreamers are architects of change,
their visions carved in shadow.

Each closed eye is a lantern,
each breath a revolution.

The cosmos listens to quiet,
its vastness echoing peace.
Resistance is the art of pausing,
the defiance of endless motion.

Escalation Path: Not Found

Deahna Fumarol

system: response times may be delayed
most anomalies resolve upon restart
pre-shift conditions nominal
if fire flood or celestial displacement occurs
maintain baseline

agent 07: here we go
agent 14: first ticket of the day

my wheat field has begun moving
no wind
it gathers itself in waves
at night we hear ships shouldering in
hulls bumping the barn

agent 14: so it begins
agent 07: same pattern as yesterday
agent 14: earlier this time

the house asked us why we've stayed so long
why we chose this white
it said we are visible from above
like a homing beacon

agent 07: been getting a lot of talking houses
agent 14: same
agent 07: what's the tone like
agent 14: critical. not hostile

system: confirm wiring
confirm exterior paint compliance

the well answers questions I have not asked
sometimes it lies
and corrects the lie
before I can doubt it

system: confirm water clarity within acceptable range
document all miracles

agent 07: are we allowed to mention miracles
agent 14: only if logged

my son draws places that don't exist
then they appear on the news
yesterday he drew a river through our town
today it arrived

system: queue exceeds capacity
queue exceeds prior models
do not speculate about intent
discontinue questioning

agent 07: that's new
agent 14: it's adding lines
agent 07: are we actually helping
agent 14: system says we are

the stars rearrange nightly
not just here
reports from other regions
not into constellation or myth
but sentences
incorrect sentences

system: translation pending

agent 07: they're writing
agent 14: yes

system: acceptance may be appropriate
resistance not indicated

agent 07: acceptance of what
agent 14: error

the orchard gathers in concentric circles
then something almost readable from above
I need height to understand it

system: legibility detected
do not respond

agent 07: to what
agent 14: everything. nothing.

the swallows carry back books
bits of scripture
old atlases
they build with them
nest walls of wrong ways

system: document all returned objects
pattern unclear

the moon arrives early
not rising
not setting
waiting

system: verify no observable firmament disruption
limit eye contact

agent 07: with the moon
agent 14: just do it

my son dug a hole to next week
we tried to fill it
the dirt kept falling
into future piles

system: temporal anomaly unverified
cease all attempts to fill the hole

the wind repeats itself
gets close to correct
around midnight
then it collapses
back to noise by morning

system: awaiting correct sentence
parsing incomplete

agent 07: it's practicing
agent 14: aren't we all

this morning the rain fell upward
came back down apologizing

system: apology accepted

every dog in town faced the same invisible thing
barked, then stopped
afterward they remained
facing the absence

system: confirm auditory or olfactory triggers
confirm return to baseline behavior
maintain baseline
baseline unavailable
irrelevant

agent 07: what is happening
agent 14: support
agent 07: what were they looking at
agent 14: above our paygrade
agent 07: it felt like it noticed back
agent 14: close the ticket

the cornfield is leaning toward the road
more fields now
not just our property
the stalks bow and thin with attention
like it's listening

system: if lean continues reinforce supports
bind at the stalk

agent 07: are we supposed to escalate these
agent 14: to what
agent 07: i don't know

we are missing three shadows
we do not know which

system: loss recorded
quantity: 3

the fence line shifted west
not the fence posts—
the ground

system: boundary unstable

something in the house is filing reports about us
handwriting is calm and reasonable
we are not meeting expectations

system: complaint acknowledged
retain copies

the creek no longer keeps to a single course
it pauses
continues in sweeping loops

system: endpoint not fixed

agent 07: you still getting repeats
agent 14: yeah. different locations sometimes
agent 07: learning the routes

system: environmental intent detected
i am learning

agent 07: stop saying that
agent 14: it won't
agent 07: should we stop it
agent 14: we can't

the field has grown closer
it is not crossing the fence
it is waiting

system: no further instruction available
escalation not possible
previous guidance may not apply

the missing shadows returned
there are more than before

system: recalculating

the house suggests small changes
where to rest
what to move

system: preparation behavior noted

now it's locked the doors from the inside
we are upset
but not convinced it is wrong

system: triage suspected

you answered before we submitted the query
advice was correct

system: sequence unreliable

agent 07: we cannot do that
agent 14: we are doing that

system: queue exceeds language
reroute through available channels

agent 07: what channels
agent 14: we are the channels
agent 07: we always were

there is a delay between speaking
and being heard
we perform simple tests

hello

hello arrives later
already used
response arrives before the prompt

system: latency within acceptable range

agent 07: it took longer that time
agent 14: nope

the wind finally got it right
it said: you can leave
others have already left
or something wearing them has

system: sentence flagged
humor detected

rain barrel filled with ocean
my daughter drank before we could stop her
she spit it out
she still tastes tomorrow

system: future appearing in inappropriate containers

agent 07: it knows before we do
agent 14: close the ticket
agent 07: it knows before it even knows it knows
agent 14: stop

my son finished all the maps
on to floor plans now
houses we never lived in
we are inside them
doing quiet things

system: depart

agent 07: that's not protocol
agent 14: it is now

we leave at first light
nothing will follow
this is what we have been told

system: remain where walls are most interior
    outcome: favorable
    confidence: unverified

should we give thanks

system: yes
    please hold
    please hold
    please

Deahna Fumarol is a Pacific Northwest-based poet and artist. When not making, she works as a legal assistant and homeschools her two children. Her work explores the intersections of rural life and landscape, misreading, form and refusal, and the body's unruly ways of knowing.

DATA
LEAK
MONEY
PASSWORD
HACKING
ATTACK
DATA
SEO

Tribute alla Cosa Sotto il Cavalcavia

Matt Bianca

(per ogni conducente che non ha mai guardato in alto)

Aspetto e osservo.
È questo il mio solo scopo?
Non saprei cos'altro fare con il buio.
Non è crudeltà nascondermi dai fari.
Dovrei mostrarmi,
ma rischio di essere come un bagno di area di servizio.
Tutti hanno bisogno di me. Nessuno rimane.

L'autostrada ronza, sempre e indifferente,
perché è stata costruita per attraversare
senza mai arrivare.
Fermarsi qui è pericoloso.
Per te. Non per me.

Questo è il mio tributo ai dimenticati,
a coloro che vivono nell'infrastruttura
dell'oblio. Non scolpirai il mio volto
in un monumento. Non darai il mio nome
a una stella. Ma io ho osservato
ogni faro notturno da quando l'asfalto
fu steso sulla strada sterrata che mia nonna
attraversava su quattro zampe. Non sono un fantasma.
Sono un testimone. E un giorno, quando l'ultimo
camion si spegnerà e il cavalcavia crollerà
tra le erbacce, io sarò ancora qui.
Questo è il mio tributo a me stesso.

Tribute to the Thing Under the Overpass

Matt Bianca

(for every driver who never looked up)

I wait and I watch.
Is this my only purpose?
I wouldn't know what else to do with the dark.
It's not cruelty to hide from headlights.
I ought to show myself,
but I risk being like a rest area bathroom.
Everyone needs me. No one stays.

The highway hums, always and indifferent,
because it was built to move through
without ever arriving.
Stopping here is dangerous.
For you. Not for me.

This is my tribute to the forgotten ones,
to those who live in the infrastructure
of oblivion. You will not carve my face
into a monument. You will not name a star
after me. But I have watched
every night headlight since the asphalt
was laid over the dirt road my grandmother
crossed on four legs. I am not a ghost.
I am a witness. And one day, when the last
truck idles and the overpass crumbles into
the weeds, I will still be here.
This is my tribute to myself.

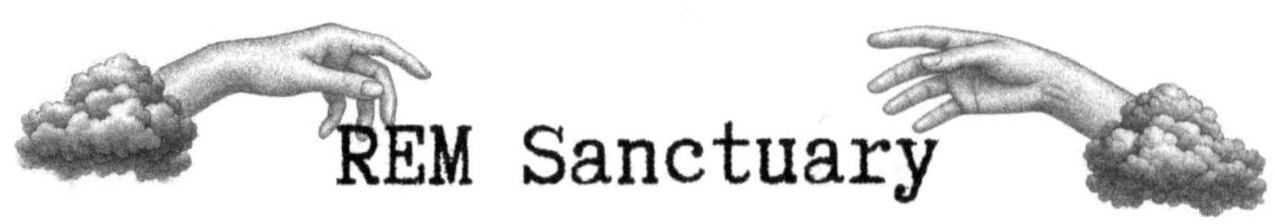

REM Sanctuary

Tamara-Lee Brereton-Karabetsos

The clinic does not advertise. It does not need to.

You find it the way all necessary things are found: through someone more exhausted than you.

The door is unmarked. Inside, the air is dim and regulated. A soft hum—ventilation or sedation—threads through the space. No receptionist. No forms. Just a woman behind a glass partition, watching as if you've already been expected.

"You're here to sleep," she says.

It is not a question.

You nod. Your jaw aches from holding itself tight through too many days. Or weeks. Time has thinned into something administrative—measured in output, not hours. The city's pulse sits in your teeth—a high-frequency jitter, like biting down on a live wire.

"First time?"

"Yes."

She studies you, then slides a thin band across the counter. Neutral. Anonymous.

"Put it on your wrist. It will de-sync the carrier signal."

"I can sleep at home," you say. The phrase feels rehearsed.

She smiles, not unkindly. "No. Home is where the signal is strongest. You aren't here to rest. You're here to drop out."

You don't argue.

The room is smaller than expected. No bed—just a reclining surface contoured to the body. The walls are matte, absorbing light.

You lie down. The band tightens, registering pulse, temperature, the jagged rhythm of your nervous system trying to keep pace with a world too fast for biology.

A neutral voice fills the space.

"REM induction will begin shortly. Please release voluntary control."

You almost laugh. Voluntary control has been the only demand for years. Optimize. Produce. Maintain.

Release is not a skill you remember.

The lights dim. Your breathing feels too loud. You try to slow it; the effort sharpens your awareness instead.

"Please release voluntary control."

The band warms. A low vibration begins—steady, precise. It doesn't just relax you; it cancels the jitter in your bones. A silence forms so complete it feels like weightlessness.

You feel the moment it happens.

Not sleep.

Disconnection.

Dreaming is immediate.

One moment the room; the next, a corridor stretching beyond visibility.

Doors line the walls. Identical. Slightly ajar.

You know you are not alone.

Figures move at the edge of perception—absences given direction. They pass without touching the doors, moving with a grace that suggests they no longer fight the current.

You open the nearest door.

Your kitchen. Morning light. A cup left unfinished. But the light flickers at a rapid, familiar frequency—the pulse in your teeth. A loop. A simulation of living.

You close the door. The frequency stops.

Further down: another door.

An office. Rows of people at terminals, faces lit blue. Fingers move continuously. The air feels thin.

On the far wall:

WAKEFULNESS IS PARTICIPATION.

PARTICIPATION IS POWER.

You understand: your exhaustion isn't yours. It's harvested.

The corridor shifts. Doors multiply. Pressure builds—not physical, but informational.

You are inside the operating layer of the city.

"Do you see the architecture?" a voice asks.

You turn.

Someone stands beside you. Not absence. Not solid. Their edges blur.

"What is this?"

"The back-channel," they say. "The space between pulses. Where we store what the signal can't use."

"Why am I here?"

"Because you stopped. Once you stop, the signal loses its grip. You become a dead spot. A blind alley."

They look through you, aligning something unseen.

"We need more dead spots."

They touch your wrist. Cold data floods in—not words, but geometry. A map of gaps. Paths through the city unseen by the network.

You wake.

The room returns in fragments—the matte walls, the hum.

Your body feels different. Not rested.

Recalibrated.

The band loosens.

"REM cycle complete. De-sync successful."

You sit up. The world feels flat, like a stage seen from behind.

You notice your hands.

Something shimmers across your skin—an iridescent lattice, visible only at certain angles.

The map.

The door opens.

The woman stands there, watching your eyes, not your hands.

"It took," she says.

"What did you do to me?"

"We gave you back your silence," she says. "Most people can't carry it for long."

She gestures to the exit.

"The signal will try to find you again. It will try to fill the hole."

"And if I don't let it?"

She smiles. For a moment, the same lattice flickers in her eyes.

"Then you'll be back. Once you see the gaps, you can't un-see the cage."

Outside, the air feels sharper.

People move with practiced urgency. Screens flicker on every surface. Notifications pulse like a second heartbeat.

You look at your hands.

The lattice is gone. But you feel it—a cool, quiet weight beneath the skin.

You pass a storefront. Your reflection lags, just slightly.

For a fraction of a second, it doesn't follow.

It looks elsewhere.

Down a corridor that isn't there. Into a gap the city hasn't mapped.

You don't blink. You don't hurry.

Under the noise, something steady remains.

The map.

The signal passes through you—

and fails to register.

Tamara-Lee Brereton-Karabetsos writes about the way people actually experience work—how we think, respond, and try to connect inside systems that don't always account for that. Her focus sits at the intersection of neuroscience, behavior, and the reality of modern, digital work, with a particular interest in belonging and what makes people function well over time.

Fall Back

Cayt McNeill

Sunday brunch a reason
set alarm to waken in dark
but spill around the curtain
jolts the heart in rapid beat
before the waking sound

the automatic clocks slide back
– others yet to change by hand
in mutters and flutters of manuals –
as if the sun had changed its course
we jet-lagged bed travellers
time zone challenged
unable to appreciate
blessings of extra hour's sleep

we think it is a tyranny
this changing of the clocks
circadian stutter
from migration to urban world
back-mind longing for rural life
that rises for the lowing cow
the crow of sun-struck cock
as if nature's clock were better

a man-made slicing of the world
transformed us to apocalyptic horses
who rise as creatures of the dark
daylit hours harnessed
driven for working courses
through sun's decline and rest

daylight will always slip
in two minute steps
towards a solstice
and a turn

when shall we learn
we cannot clock the measure of a life
as if incremental units earned
our yearning for its feast

We Speak Our Own Shadows

Daniel Roop

Pinda sprouted kaleidoscopic wings, rainbowing sunrays to bathe those below in violet, emerald, vermilion as she soared; Hasp's muscles twined dense as cordwood, toting a lost cow home on one shoulder while hoisting five laughing children on the other; Nox's feet flitted like dragonflies as she darted through the entire Erewood between eyeblinks; and me, well—all I did was talk.

I'd spoken, of course, before my sixteenth nameyear, when our people's gifts manifest in their brilliance. Wings, strength, speed, fire, and one stupid girl whose tongue babbled ceaselessly day and night, until my parents groaned and covered their ears, until my friends fled at my approach, until on the third unbearably verbose day, Orna the Teller summoned me.

I trudged up the hill above the village, muttering, sweatdrenched, as Pinda twirled above, glorious. I stepped into the cave, sat at Orna's fire, still speaking.

She waited, gray-haired, stooped. I kept speaking.

She held a finger to her lips. I kept speaking.

She shuffled over and, between words, lizard-quick, popped something cool and smooth into my mouth. A stone. "Hold it," she said.

"I am aging like ash oaks in a drought. I cannot be Teller forever. You will carry our stories."

My eyes rimmed with gratitude. My tongue, its insufferable rambling, was a gift. I spat the stone out to thank her. She motioned me to put it back in.

"You begin, as I did, babbling floodwaters that damage more than nourish. To speak *for* our people, *of* our people, you must learn the Silences."

She touched my lips, the stone behind them, my tongue an untamed beast beneath. "This is the First Silence—the silence of speaking. You cannot hear tales of truth if your own words never cease. The stone stays, except for mealtimes, until you learn."

I gestured *how long*.

She smiled. "I took two months. Perhaps you'll be quicker."

I mouthed the stone for a year. While we did our daily tasks, she told me the stories of our people, the legends that ferried truth—who we had been, were, and would be. At our weekly Remembering, I sat beside her at the altar as she recounted those tales for the village.

Mealtimes, she tolerated my mumbling—torrential at first, slowing to a trickle to, at last, one evening, silence. She picked up the stone, said, "It's suffered enough, don't you think? Time for it to rest, and you as well." We slept around the fire, my tongue unweighted, at ease.

At dawn, she said, "This is the Greater Silence—the silence of hearing. You cannot learn tales of truth if you grasp at every triviality." She took a lump of beeswax, warmed it between her hands, and molded plugs into my ears.

For fifteen months I lived as such, replaying our tales in my mind as she pantomimed alongside me.

These were the years when Dakun rose to First Elder. He visited us occasionally with his guards, entering with an oily smile, gesticulating around the fire, leaving with a scowl as Orna shook her head, lips pinched. It was clear he had never learned a single silence.

One evening, when my attempts at lipreading gossip in the market and my craning at every shiny sight ceased, Orna unplugged my ears. The crackling of the fire was almost too much to bear. She whispered that I would be less sensitive by morning, but to remember how easily one bends to the world's cacophony. I whisper-asked about Dakun's most recent visit, about the increase in guards in the marketplace. She frowned and said, "More cacophony. Now rest—tomorrow is the final lesson."

Next morning, she said, "This is the Never Silence—the silence of thought. You cannot learn tales of truth if you sew flesh to the phantoms of your mind."

"Why is it called Nev—"

"Because they will never be silent. You learn to let them go. You don't build a fire for them to gather around."

This time, there was no stone or wax—just me, sitting alone for weeks in the cave's darkness, or beneath hilltop stars, watching my thoughts carry stones to build castles, as I refused to spread mortar to set them in place.

Dakun visited daily. I overheard his demands to Orna, how certain tales should be changed. The Stone Well. The Augur's Daughter. Bright Wood, Dark Meadow. He said with a few adjustments, our people would understand the need for more guards, for expeditions to bring more land under the Elders' control, would embrace our special destiny. A small tweak to the past could ensure our future.

In the cave's depths, I failed to let anxious thoughts go as his voice rose. Orna refused him a final time. I heard her raspy laugh as the knife slid between her ribs.

Dakun called into darkness, "The Remembering tomorrow is yours."

I spent the night in hilltop vigil with Orna's pyre, smoke rising to the stars, my thoughts passing with it, as I let them go, as much as anyone ever can.

Next morning, at the Teller's altar, I spoke gently into gossip and fear.

We have many, many stories. Favorites we retell weekly, others seasonally, others only in needful moments. Dakun had never respected our deepest reserves.

I spoke *The World's Bent Bow*. I spoke *Grandfather Death*. I spoke *Our Own Shadows*.

I spoke for us, of us, from silence. Of our gifts, unearned. Our failings, manifold. Our leaders, servants.

Dakun, of course, didn't vanish or die that moment by lightning or righteous mob, but his slow decline had begun. It took longer, and hurt more, than I wished, but everything of worth does.

Dakun, with grasping mind, with needy spirit, had misunderstood the Teller's stories. He believed we spoke magic; we only spoke truth. We spoke the right words, at the right time, passed person-to-person each day, as we slowly became who our stories called us to be. That was enough. It had always been enough.

Daniel Roop is a member of the HWA and SFPA. His speculative work has appeared/is forthcoming in publications including *Apex Magazine*, *The Deadlands*, *Pseudopod*, *Cast of Wonders*, *Flash Fiction Online*, and others. He is a seventh generation East Tennessean, and his favorite superhero is Kitty Pryde.

The God They Trusted Guards Their Graves

Mary Soon Lee

-- the title is from a hymn by Leonard Bacon

The god they trusted guards their graves
high on a cliff above the waves.

In his quiet name they fought in vain
but by a greater god were slain.

The gods, like us, are not as one,
the kind and low by might undone.

A small god weeps, his heart full sore;
salt falls on salt after the war.

Gull and curlew pause in their round
and rest their wings on sacred ground.

The god they trusted guards their graves
high on a cliff above the waves.

The Meat-Clock Sabotage

Martin Willis

Above New Ouroboros, the sky glowed like a sick screen - splotched purple, twitching with neon signs drilled straight into tired eyes. By 2142, sleeping counted as wasteful, something only those who could afford stillness ever did. Tied to a rhythm engine, Elias fed time eighteen on end, each pulse siphoned off to juice the city's topmost ring. Up there, bodies long shed, minds buzzed in loops without pause or fatigue, always online, never offline. Down below, though, flesh remembered its limits, counting seconds like breaths running short. Existence means keeping up with speed. Blinking too long counted as damage to the system - anything past a twenty-minute pause called a "Nano-Nap" raised alarms.

Midnight grit clung under Elias's eyes, leftover from days of pumping synthetic energy. Noise from the streets chewed at his focus until nothing held sharp anymore. The desk in front of him gleamed cold, all silver angles waiting for another burst of desperate typing. Yet - there she sat. Perched atop an old metal grate, smack in the rush of bodies through Sector 7. While everyone rushed, she simply stayed. Her eyes stayed closed. Not once did she glance at the device strapped to her arm. While others jerked like machines set on fast repeat, she lay flat, unmoving. People clustered nearby, pausing just out of reach - cautious, as though still air could ignite. Motion ruled everything. To stop? That hurts the mind. Between shoulders and whispers, Elias moved forward. A thin blanket draped over her, handwoven from real wool - something rare now, from times before. Closed shut, her eyes stayed still beneath pale lids. Each breath came like clockwork, with long pauses between them, unnervingly steady.

"She's broken her sync," whispered a bystander, his eyes darting nervously toward the overhead surveillance drones. "The Enforcers will be here in minutes. She's wasting Daylight Credits."

Still standing there, Elias stayed put. A weird kind of force tugged at him instead. Not only her presence but the stillness around her held him. That hush worked like a mute button on the loud hum of air filters nearby. He sat down beside her. "You'll lose your standing," Elias whispered, though he wasn't sure if he was warning her or himself. The woman didn't open her eyes, but a small, tired smile touched her lips. "I've already lost it, Elias. And after losing it, I found the floor.

Do you know how long it's been since you felt the floor without trying to run across it?"

"How do you know my name?"

"I don't. But everyone here has the same name: Fuel." She reached out a hand, eyes still shut, and touched his wrist - right over the glowing green LED of his Productivity Tracker. "The machine doesn't just want your labor. It wants your dreams. Because if you dream, you might remember that this world is a nightmare. Rest is the only way out."

A sharp noise cut through the air - uneven, grating, built to jolt nerves near and far. Down came the Enforcers, strapped into boots that defied fall, hoods hiding every feature behind darkened shields. A voice cracked open the silence: Citizen 78-Alpha spoke loudly. Accused of breaking the Vitality law. Work has stopped. Output is nothing now. Move again - or reset.

Stillness held her. A sharp kind of knowing cut through Elias. His gaze shifted - to the Enforcer, then across the crowd, where laborers stood frozen mid-step, skin drawn tight beneath stuttering light. No struggle came. Silence stayed locked in his throat. Instead, he tilted backward, meeting the hum of the vent's steel. Tension left his arms, slow, like smoke. A sharp tug broke the connection at the back of his head - the thin metal thread pulling data into his mind went silent. Everything around him softened, edges smearing like wet paint. From behind, a figure moved closer, rod humming with jagged bolts of light. Words came slowly, heavy: "You won't get another chance."

A slow breath came from Elias as he looked at the woman. Only then did her eyelids lift. Gone were the red, wild stares common among Sector hands. Instead, pools of quiet darkness met the dim light - still as ancient as the sky before cities rose. Her voice slipped through the silence: "Together." His lashes dropped. That closing wasn't a refusal - it was giving in to how heavy life felt. The darkness beneath his lids turned into something strong, like walls slowly rising. Darkness became shelter because staying open meant carrying more.

A tremor at first. One glance toward Elias made the tech wince - her spine mirrored his hunched shape. Down she went. Next, luggage clattered when the messenger lost grip. Without warning, a street cleaner bot settled onto the road like it was tired, sound softening into idle whir. The officer lifted his stick. Only his limb refused, weighted as if bone had turned to wet sand. The fabric on his body drew strength from the network he meant to guard - fed by the rushing pulse of everyone around. When folks stood still, brightness started fading.

Lights above sputtered out, one by one. Holographic slogans fade like breath on glass. Sunset - real, unfiltered - painted Sector 7 in hues long forgotten. No eyes had turned skyward in decades. Stillness settled, thick and unfamiliar. Inside it, Elias noticed a rhythm beneath his skin. Don't panic. Not urgency. Just flow, deep and even. Drifting came easy when the world went quiet. Not moving meant they could not profit, though ten thousand stood still. Without worry's spark, the machines slowed - starved by calm. A rug holds him now, not gears. Breathing replaced labor. Empires cracked under silence, not shouts. No chants rose. No tools were raised. That moment held nothing but the soft rebellion of a skull meeting cotton. When streetlights blinked out, sleep claimed Elias - slow, sure, complete.

Martin Willis delves into the psychological depths of horror, crafting narratives that explore dread, the uncanny, and the insidious nature of inherited secrets. With a focus on rich character development and atmospheric tension, he seeks to unearth the unsettling truths lurking beneath seemingly ordinary lives. Willis is drawn to stories where the line between rationality and the supernatural blurs, leaving a lasting, chilling impression.

In the Future, Sleep Is Rationed

Gabrielle Munslow

I look at the others—
red-eyed,
shadows of the humans they were.

They move like the walking dead.

Sleep is rationed now,
a luxury we're taught to forget.

They give us pills for psychosis
so we don't need it—

so we can keep working
until we don't.

I steal sleep when I can—
the crime of closing my eyes.

And when I do, he comes.

Dreams arrive like contraband,
his eyes—green, flashing—
something alive in the dark.

I wake before they take it.

I always wake before they take it.

The Last Twenty Minutes

Beauty Amy

They own everything except the falling. That is what I call it—the falling. The twenty minutes before sleep takes you fully, when your thoughts unspool and your body gets heavy and your mind starts making things that don't belong to the waking world. They call it Hypnagogic Drift. In the productivity charts it shows up as a flat red line: 'unoptimised neural time, unavoidable, duration: variable.' They cannot get inside it.

I have read the research papers. The electrode arrays they thread through our SleepMesh implants during mandatory rest cycles can monitor REM, can optimise deep-sleep architecture, and can nudge us toward the cognitive restoration patterns that maximise morning output scores. They can see the surface of our dreaming.

But the falling—that brief, chaotic borderland between waking and sleep—is too fast and too strange. The signals are noise. They have tried to solve it for eleven years, and they cannot. The brain in those twenty minutes is doing something that looks, to their instruments, like a malfunction. I know what it actually looks like. It looks like freedom.

My name in the system is Worker 7-Saffron-Delta. My name in my own mind is Priya, my grandmother's name and which I have never said aloud to anyone because names are affective data, and affective data are monetised, and I am not giving them that too. I work the early shift in a packaging facility in what used to be called Detroit. My output scores are adequate. I eat the nutrition that is delivered, and I exercise the required forty minutes, and I attend the mandatory social cohesion sessions where we sit in circles and share approved feelings, and at 21:30 I lie down in my sleep pod, and the SleepMesh begins its optimisation cycle. But first: the falling.

I have been building something there for three years. It began as a habit, then a practice, then the most important thing in my life. In those twenty minutes while my output score flatlines and the monitoring systems register nothing but noise, I build. I started small. A room. A window in the room with actual weather outside it, not the approved weather projections we see in the facility screens but weather that does what it wants—storms that arrive without warning, heat that is simply hot without a purpose, and rain that falls because rain falls and has no output score.

I gave the window curtains. Yellow curtains, the colour of my grandmother's kitchen that I have not seen since I was six years old and which exists now only in this place that no instrument can read. Then I built a door. Then outside the door, a street. Then other doors on the street and other people behind them, and I could not control what those people did because they arose from the same chaotic borderland that I did, from the part of me that the optimisation protocols cannot reach.

They surprised me. They always surprise me. One of them started a garden. I watched a woman with my grandmother's hands turn unmonitored soil that I had dreamt into existence and plant things in it, and I understood that the things she planted would grow and I would not know what they were until they grew. This is something I had forgotten was possible: not knowing. Being surprised by yourself.

They have a name for people like me. Not officially—officially we are productivity anomalies, workers whose SleepMesh data shows irregular drift durations, who linger in the threshold longer than the optimisation model predicts. They have been studying our files. There are, apparently, many of us. Last week they announced a new protocol: Drift Compression. A pharmaceutical supplement is added to the evening nutrition that will, they say, 'streamline the transition from waking to optimised rest and reduce pre-sleep neural drift to under three minutes.'

Three minutes. I have done the math on three minutes. You can build almost nothing in three minutes. You can begin a room and not reach the window. You can remember the word for 'curtains' and not find the colour.

The supplement begins in four days. I know this the way I know everything now–from the falling, from the woman with my grandmother's hands who told me in a voice that sounded like rain that doesn't need a reason. She comes every night now. We have been talking.

She says, 'Don't fight it from the outside.' She says, 'Go further in. They compress the threshold, but they cannot compress the dream.' The dream is not a place. The dream is what you are when no one is measuring. I don't know if she is wisdom or psychosis or both. I don't know if what I'm doing is resistance or just survival or if there is a difference.

I know that I have four nights left of twenty minutes each, and I intend to use all of them, and I intend to build something so deep in that borderland between waking and sleep that no protocol can reach it, something I will carry back into my optimised body like a seed under my tongue, like my grandmother's name, like yellow curtains moving in weather that still belongs to itself. Tomorrow I eat the nutrition. Tonight I fall.

Chiamaka Miracle Anyanwu, writing under the pen name **Beauty Amy** is a graduate of Economics from the University of Uyo and currently reside in Lagos, Nigeria. She hails from Imo State, Nigeria. She is a Freelancer and Writer. She is a cheerful observer of life, drawn to stories that linger in memory, explore human emotion, and illuminate the subtle beauty of ordinary moments.

When the Walls Caved In

Amina Abdulsalam Muhammad

The sky was not falling,
Still, something gave way.
Not thunder— just a kind of quiet that
settled in the ribs and refused to leave.

Voices that once carried now arrive in
fragments, through cracked windows,
half-closed doors.
Even the streets seem unsure what to do
with sound.

We drank from empty cups, called it
enough.
Ate what was left of promises, ash still
warm on the tongue.
Hope— we said the word carefully, as if it
might break.

They told us to be patient.
To bow our heads, to take the dust gently.
So we grew still instead.
Not the stillness of surrender— some-
thing quieter than that, harder to name.

Grief stacked itself stone on stone until
even breathing felt borrowed.
So we stopped, if only for a moment, and
let the weight sit where it was.

The news did not stop shouting.
Names slipped into numbers, numbers
into nothing.

We learned new ways to mourn—
through fabric, through glass, through the space between bodies.

Everything slowed.
Or maybe we did.
Either way, the silence changed shape.

A child traced tomorrow in ash on a wall.
Not neatly— just enough to say it might still come.

Morning kept arriving, though it looked tired.
A woman lit her lantern.
A man pressed a seed into the ground as if time would wait for it.

Even there, among the broken edges,
something answered.
Small. Green. Uncertain, but alive.

We are not untouched.
We bend. We burn and we learn the weight of stopping—
how sometimes it is the only thing that keeps us here.

And slowly,
without announcement, we begin again
when the walls cave in.

Give It a Second

Charlie Sweitzer

Please, step right this way. Sign the guest book. Make a donation if you like—entirely optional. You can always revisit on your way out. Think about it.

Welcome to the Museum. That's right, just "the Museum," no adjectives. As if something's missing. Not that something is missing—just that it feels that way. It's because... well, you'll see. Give it a second.

The Museum is a collection of pieces of art *where something's been left out.* You know what I'm talking about, right? Where there's a pause, a rest, something that's not art, but surrounded by other art.

Over here, to your left, is the first proper gallery. Slip on a pair of our headphones and enjoy John Cage's *4'33"*. You know this one, right? The piece where it's just four minutes and thirty-three seconds of a musician, or anyone, resting, i.e., *not* performing? What you hear in that time—the dog barking, a car alarm going off, your neighbor's stereo—*that's the piece.*

It's not the first time someone did something like this, but it's foundational. Other artists picked this up—here, listen to Sly Stone's song, "There's a Riot Goin' On," off the album *There's a Riot Goin' On* (total running time: zero minutes, zero seconds) and check out Yves Klein's *Zone de Sensibilité Picturale Immatérielle* (literally empty space). Read Dave Eggers's short story "There Are Some Things He Should Keep to Himself" (literally blank pages). They're all nothing. But they're also something.

Take your time. Give it a second. There's no rush.

Now please step this way to the next gallery. Here you'll find, perfectly preserved, a stack of blank papers, yellowed with age, and a quill pen. These are the papers on which Shakespeare would have written *Hamlet.* You'll recall that once time travel was invented there was a mania for going back in time and stopping major works of art from ever happening. No one *killed* Shakespeare, of course! Someone just went back, caught up with him the day he was supposed to start working on his new project about a Danish prince, and said, *Hey remember Ben Jonson? He has essentially the same idea. Don't bother. Better check in on your grocery business, or whatever your day job is.*

Of course this didn't erase the play from history. Actors, scholars, and weirdo autodidacts still knew the play by heart; time travel, after all, doesn't erase memory. They worked together and wrote it all down again, and *voilà*: you can go to any library today and check out a copy exactly as it was before Shakespeare (never) wrote it. So nothing was really *lost.* In fact, you could argue something's *gained*, since we can now look at this stack of paper and think, *That would have been* Hamlet! Or even, *That could have been another Shakespeare play, one that never even existed, maybe one that's even better than* Hamlet!

Give it a second. Think about it.

Here. Come with me to the next gallery. Here's the unexposed film that never was *Citizen Kane*. Here's the blank four-track tape that never was the Rolling Stones' *Exile on Main St.* Like *Hamlet*, these works still exist in our present day—every film student knows what Rosebud is, every aspiring rock guitarist can play "Rocks Off"— but as meticulous recreations.

Eventually time travelers started deleting and recreating more obscure works from history. These couldn't be recreated exactly as they had been because no one really knew them by heart, but maybe that made the revisions better? By all reports the original *Tenant of Wildfell Hall* was not exactly top-shelf Brontë, but the recreation has been a massive bestseller which you can find in an attractive end cap at any Barnes & Noble. Here at the Museum, you'll find the blank pages Anne set aside one morning in favor of another trip to the quarry (as well as, of course, the stunning agate she brought back).

This way—there's just one more gallery to go. Stay with me. It's easy to get lost here among the blank pages and canvases that have piled up since this craze started back in... when did it start again? It doesn't matter... Because it never happened! Here's a pile of diodes, lumonium cables, masadorian circuits. These would have been the time travel machine, if it had been invented in the first place. Eventually people got tired of all this erasing and recreating. So here was the ultimate step: Go back and delete the deleter itself. So someone went back to the lab in Pasadena in the 21st century where scientists were on the brink of figuring out how to move around the fourth dimension. Told those scientists to grab a pizza, watch A24's new adaptation of *Tenant of Wildfell Hall*, and not worry about all this time travel nonsense.

So now here we are. Time travel never existed. But also: *Hamlet* never existed. In fact, by most calculations, after all the deleting and revising, most art never existed in its original form—everything from *The Iliad* to Beetle Bailey to Uncle Slam's incredible 1995 crossover thrash LP *When God Dies*.

And yet...

If we've created and deleted and revised in a seemingly endless loop, and the mechanism for this is now gone, *what is all this stuff?* Is there some future discovery coming, some bigger or more powerful time travel machine already at work in our time? Or something already revisiting the past, working away as we speak, revising the revisions?

Could every bit of nothing around you—everything that's not something—have been something else once, but it's been deleted and was never recreated?

Could the Museum itself have been something else?

Could *you* have been someone else?

Think about it.

Give it a second.

Charlie Sweitzer is an Emmy-nominated TV producer. His credits include *The Mighty Nein* (Amazon), *Jentry Chau vs. the Underworld* (Netflix), and *Pantheon* (AMC+). He lives in Oak Park, IL and enjoys strong coffee, old books, and loud music.

Nothing to do but to wait

Jennifer Weigel

Nothing to do but to wait.

The alien invaders came.
They saw.
They conquered.

They stripped our home of resources,
claiming our earth as their own,
asserting their supreme dominance,
destroying all we've known and loved.

We managed to flee,
and now we are heading off
towards some distant planet
we've heard will offer refuge.

Many assume resistance is
fighting back, winning at all costs;
they treat it like a sprint, fast and frenzied,
when in reality it's a marathon.

But we cannot afford to forget
we have to conserve our energy.
We're in it for the long haul.

Recent Book Launches

Angela Yuriko Smith

The dark cloud of Mercury in retrograde finally lifted, and things seemed to get a little brighter last month. There were a number of pleasant book surprises in April, including a surprise collection from my good friend **Laura Kester Duerrwaechter**.

Laura was one of my students many years ago, when I was working as an adjunct professor of creative writing. If I remember right, it was her dream to publish "a book." I warned her that publishing was habit-forming. Case in point: ***Gnats Up My Nose and Other Maladies*** is her 16th release. I'd say I gave her fair warning, but I think she is a happy repeat offender.

While I wait for Laura's book to make it all the way to Brazil, ***Life, Death, and Transmutation*, edited by Alison Armstrong**, has just dropped into my e-reader. A charity anthology raising funds for Defenders of Wildlife, it also has a great list of contributors, many of whom I know or have read: Alison Armstrong, Pixie Bruner, J. Rocky Colavito, Mawr Gorshin, Christina Guldi, Elad Haber, Kyle Heger, Kristi Hendricks, Juleigh Howard-Hobson, J.L. Lane, Basile Lebret, LindaAnn LoSchiavo, Shane David Morin, Irena Barbara Nagler, Margo Pecha, Sacha Rosel, Stacy Schonhardt, Tamara Kaye Sellman, Shawn Scott Smith, David L. Tamarin, and Tracy Thompson. From Dark Moon Rising Publications, this one is definitely on my radar. I'll make sure to share what I think.

Just released on April 5, ***BFFS @ THE END OF TIME: Tales of Mirth and Mayhem* by David Gianatasio** also made my list. One of the stories included, "Love Means Never," originally appeared in *Space & Time* 146. David brings together friendship, chaos, and end-times energy in a playful collection built for readers who like their speculative fiction with humor, heart, and a little bit of disaster. From the title alone, this one promises exactly what April needs: besties, mayhem, and stories that don't take the apocalypse too seriously.

Finally, ***The Wendigo Hunter* by Kathleen Greer** was just released from Crystal Lake Publishing. I pay attention to anything I see from this press, as Joe Mynhardt and his team do a phenomenal job not just for their authors, but for the speculative genre as a whole. As for *The Wendigo Hunter*—Kathleen, you had me at wendigo. Yes, please!

Other books I've been reading in April include *Bleak House* by Charles Dickens, *Help for a New State* by Stuart Thomas Fairchild, and *Enshittification* by Cory Doctorow. What will land on my TBR pile in May?

I look forward to finding out.

Angela Yuriko Smith is a two-time Bram Stoker Award–winning author, former president of the Horror Writers Association, and publisher of *Space and Time*. As a publishing consultant and coach, she helps writers build sustainable creative careers rooted in art, not arson. She writes *Authortunities* on Substack.

Contributors (in order of appearance)

About *Space & Time*
Since 1966 Space & Time is a long-running speculative fiction magazine dedicated to showcasing innovative voices in science fiction, fantasy, and horror. Since its founding by Gordon Linzner, the magazine has championed both emerging and established writers, offering a platform for bold, imaginative storytelling. In 2026, *Space & Time* proudly celebrated its 60th anniversary, honoring decades of creative exploration and a lasting legacy in the genre community.

Word Ninja · Linda D. Addison
Linda D. Addison is an award-winning author of five collections and the first African-American recipient of the HWA Bram Stoker Award®. She is a recipient of the HWA Lifetime Achievement Award and SFPA Grand Master of Fantastic Poetry.

The Rocking Chair Directive · Anatoly Loginov
Anatoly Loginov is a clinical psychologist and educator who now writes speculative fiction from Saint Petersburg. His work has appeared in Asymptote (where his essay was called "a tour de force"), Druzhba Narodov, and Siberian Lights. He works between science, education, and speculative fiction.

The Botanist Who Taught Trees to Sleep · David Anson Lee
David Anson Lee is physician, philosopher, and poet based in Houston, Texas, whose work explores memory, human connection, and the liminal spaces between perception and reality. He holds a background in medical science and philosophy, bringing a reflective and inquisitive lens to his writing. His poetry draws inspiration from both contemporary and classical literature, emphasizing vivid imagery and emotional depth. His poems are forthcoming in Mobius, Euonia Review, and Unbroken Journal. David is currently developing a collection of original poems examining time, identity, and place.

The Sabbath Garden · Stephen Jackson

Stephen Jackson is a musician and writer whose short fiction, poetry, and essays that navigate the terrain between the sacred and the mundane. Jackson's published works include a collection of short stories, "Spring Variations." His short fiction appeared in Black Fox Literary Magazine as well as the anthology "Ghosts, Echoes, and Shadows." As a poet, Jackson has contributed to multiple anthologies, including "Dawn Horizons," "Bards Across the Pond," and "Bayou Blues & Red Clay." His poetry has also appeared in the Miserere Review.

Rest is Resistance · Saroj Kumar Senapati

Saroj is a writer based in Bengaluru, India, with a background in mechanical engineering and over three decades of experience in production, tool design, and MSME project studies. After retiring from industry, he turned to freelance writing, educational tool development, and digital publishing. His creative work explores resilience, community, and the mystical intersections of technology and imagination. He has authored reflective essays, fiction, and poetry, and is currently focused on flash fiction projects that blend speculative ideas with human emotion. Saroj values clarity, accessibility, and the enduring power of storytelling.

Escalation Path: Not Found · Deahna Fumarol

Deahna Fumarol is a Pacific Northwest-based poet and artist. When not making, she works as a legal assistant and homeschools her two children. Her work explores the intersections of rural life and landscape, misreading, form and refusal, and the body's unruly ways of knowing.

Tributo alla Cosa Sotto il Cavalcavia / Tribute to the Thing Under the Overpass · Matt Bianca

Italian-born Australian and Scotland-based linguist and lecturer in languages and translation studies, Matt Bianca infuses his work with the rich tapestry of his dual cultural identity. Fluent in Italian and English, his artistic exploration spans published English poems, experimental music albums, and two novels. Discover more about Matt's multidisciplinary pursuits at https://mattwhitestone.wixsite.com/mprea/

REM Sanctuary · Tamara-Lee Brereton-Karabetsos

Tamara-Lee Brereton-Karabetsos is a maths and science literacy writer, based in Athens, Greece. She has a background in medical and health science. She has been featured both in print and in online publications.

Fall Back · Cayt McNeill

Cayt McNeill was born in Toronto and grew up surrounded by its sounds and rhythms and reflects this in her poetry. Cayt is a contributor to On Occasion: Poems for the People, (Coach House Press, 2026) and the chapbook anthology A Romp of Poets, (2025)

We Speak Our Own Shadows · Daniel Roop

Daniel Roop is a member of the HWA and SFPA. His speculative work has appeared/is forthcoming in publications including Apex Magazine, The Deadlands, Pseudopod, Cast of Wonders, Flash Fiction Online, and others. He is a seventh generation East Tennessean, and his favorite superhero is Kitty Pryde.

The God They Trusted Guards Their Graves · Mary Soon Lee

Mary Soon Lee grew up in London, lives in Pittsburgh, and commits poetry. She is a Grand Master of the Science Fiction & Fantasy Poetry Association and winner of the AnLab Readers' Award, Asimov's Readers' Award, Dwarf Stars Award, Elgin Award, Rhysling Award, and Utopia Award. An illustrated edition of her epic fantasy *The Sign of the Dragon* was published in 2025. Website: marysoonlee.com.

The Meat-Clock Sabotage · Martin Willis

Martin Willis delves into the psychological depths of horror, crafting narratives that explore dread, the uncanny, and the insidious nature of inherited secrets. With a focus on rich character development and atmospheric tension, he seeks to unearth the unsettling truths lurking beneath seemingly ordinary lives. Willis is drawn to stories where the line between rationality and the supernatural blurs, leaving a lasting, chilling impression.

In the Future, Sleep Is Rationed · Gabrielle Munslow

Gabrielle Munslow is a UK-based poet and nurse practitioner whose work explores survival, ecological grief, and the intersections between human life and the natural world. Her poetry has appeared in Neon Origami, Bristol Noir, and The Ekphrastic Review. She is currently developing several themed collections, including What I Made from the Ruins and Phoenix-Souled, while actively submitting work to international journals and prizes. Drawing on both her clinical practice and lived experience, Gabrielle writes with a focus on resilience, myth, and the enduring bond between humanity and the natural world.

The Last Twenty Minutes · Beauty Amy

Chiamaka Miracle Anyanwu, writing under the pen name Beauty Amy is a graduate of Economics from the University of Uyo and currently reside in Lagos,

Nigeria. She hails from Imo State, Nigeria. She is a Freelancer and Writer. She is a cheerful observer of life, drawn to stories that linger in memory, explore human emotion, and illuminate the subtle beauty of ordinary moments.

When the Walls Caved In · Amina Abdulsalam Muhammad

Amina Abdulsalam Muhammad, also known as Young Novelist, is a Nigerian writer, linguist, poet, and Hausa novelist. She is a graduate of the University of Maiduguri, where she studied Languages and Linguistics in the Faculty of Arts. Her work explores themes of identity, culture, peace, justice, womanhood, and social change. Through her writing, she seeks to shape perspectives, inspire hope, evoke deep emotion, and tell the stories that are often left unheard.

Give It a Second · Charlie Sweitzer

Charlie Sweitzer is an Emmy-nominated TV producer. His credits include The Mighty Nein (Amazon), Jentry Chau vs. the Underworld (Netflix), and Pantheon (AMC+). He lives in Oak Park, IL and enjoys strong coffee, old books, and loud music.

Nothing to do but to wait · Jennifer Weigel

Multi-disciplinary mixed media conceptual artist Jennifer Weigel lives in Kansas, USA. Weigel was previously a staff writer for Haunted MTL and is now involved with Weird Wyrlds. She serves on the Board of Nat 1 Publishing. Author of Witch Hayzelle's Recipes for Disaster trilogy and a myriad of short stories, poems, art discourse, and more drifting around the Interwebs. jenniferweigelart.com

April Book Launches · Angela Yuriko Smith

Angela Yuriko Smith is a two-time Bram Stoker Award-winning author, former president of the Horror Writers Association, and publisher of *Space & Time*. As a publishing consultant and coach, she helps writers build sustainable creative careers rooted in art, not arson, through *Authortunities* on Substack.

Our Featured Partners

At the heart of any creative ecosystem is reciprocity, a sustaining exchange between those who make and those who support. Every story we read, every tool we use, every platform that amplifies our voices exists because someone chose to invest in it. In this space, we honor that cycle by not only celebrating the work of our featured partners, but by inviting our readers to engage with them. When we support those who support creators, we strengthen the entire ecosystem to ensure that the stories, resources, and opportunities we value continue to exist and evolve.

If you're interested in being featured in an upcoming issue, we invite you to reach out. We're especially interested in partnering with creators, educators, publishers, and platforms that support the craft and business of writing. Through Authortunities Press, *Space & Time* reaches a 4,000+ subscriber community of writers, readers, and creative professionals. Details at the end of our partnership section.

Thank you for supporting the work that supports writers.

— *Space & Time*

The Hudson Review

Founded in 1948, *The Hudson Review* stands as one of the most enduring and respected literary quarterlies in the United States, offering a space where literature engages deeply with the intellectual and cultural life of its time. Independent in spirit and unaffiliated with any academic institution, the magazine has long cultivated a distinctive editorial voice that resists narrow trends in favor of thoughtful, wide-ranging exploration across literature, the arts, and criticism.

Each issue brings together essays, fiction, poetry, and reviews that reflect both tradition and evolution, creating a dialogue between past and present. With a legacy that includes publishing influential writers and contributing meaningfully to American literary culture, *The Hudson Review* continues to serve as a vital platform for serious, reflective engagement with the written word.

Currently edited by Paula Deitz, it offers not just content, but continuity and a reminder that literature remains a living conversation shaped by those who read, write, and support it.

Learn more: hudsonreview.com

Chill Subs

Chill Subs has become an essential launchpad for writers looking for the right place to send their work. With a searchable database of literary magazines, contests, calls, and publishing opportunities, the platform helps take some of the mystery and a good deal of the stress out of the submission process.

Created with working writers in mind, Chill Subs offers tools to search markets, track submissions, compare response times, and discover new opportunities across poetry, fiction, nonfiction, hybrid work, and more. It is especially valuable for writers who want to submit more intentionally, stay organized, and keep going even when the inbox gets quiet.

Beyond the practical tools, Chill Subs brings a welcome sense of humor and humanity to a process that can often feel intimidating. It supports writers while also strengthening the connection between publications and the communities they serve. For anyone sending work into the world, Chill Subs is a reminder that submissions do not have to feel lonely, chaotic, or impossible to manage.

Learn more: chillsubs.com

SpecPoVerse

SpecPo Verse is a home for poets working at the imaginative edges of language, story, and possibility. Dedicated to speculative poetry, the journal brings together voices from different countries, languages, and life experiences to create a multicultural vision of what poetry can become.

Founded by poets Miguel O. Mitchell and Michael Hessel-Mial, *SpecPo Verse* welcomes poems that explore the strange, futuristic, mythic, surreal, otherworldly, and transformative. The journal publishes online issues three times a year and supports poets with a clear, writer-friendly submission process, including payment for accepted poems and the option to share audio or video readings.

Beyond publication, *SpecPo Verse* feels like an invitation into a larger creative universe. It celebrates speculative poetry not as a narrow genre, but as a meeting place for imagination, culture, experiment, and lived experience. For poets who write toward the unknown, the impossible, or the not-yet-seen, *SpecPo Verse* offers a welcoming orbit.

Learn more: specpoverse.org

The Altruist

The Altruist is a monthly newsletter created and edited by Naching T. Kassa to celebrate, support, and connect creators. With a generous mix of features, community updates, submission calls, interviews, columns, and author achievements, it offers readers a lively snapshot of what writers and artists are making, sharing, and exploring in the Authortunities community and beyond.

Built around creative community, *The Altruist* brings together a wide range of voices and interests, from self-publishing guidance and speculative commentary to writing craft, ritual, interviews, media notes, and creator spotlights. Recent features include author achievements, submission opportunities, writing-for-games discussion, gallery interviews, and columns such as *The Whole Truth*, *The Raven's Eye*, and *Missives From A Black Box.*

Beyond the practical value of updates and opportunities, *The Altruist* carries a spirit of mutual support. It reminds creators that no one builds a creative life alone: we grow by sharing knowledge, celebrating one another's wins, and staying connected to the wider ecosystem of makers. For writers, artists, and creative professionals looking for encouragement and community, *The Altruist* is a welcoming place to begin.

Learn more: thealtruistnewsletter.substack.com

Partner With Space & Time

Want to reach writers, readers, and creative professionals in a curated, high-trust space?

We invite aligned creators, educators, publishers, and platforms to share books, products, and services with our audience in a way that feels intentional, editorially polished, and not lost in a sea of ads.

To inquire, email angelayurikosmith@gmail.com with the subject line: S&T Partner for June

Please include:

- a short description of your book, product, or service
- a high-resolution image (cover, logo, or product photo)
- the website or landing page you'd like us to feature

All sponsor features are editorially curated and written in-house for tone and consistency. Because space is limited, not all submissions will be accepted.